*For Jamie*
~J.S.
*For Toby and Charlie*
~T.W.

ISBN 0-590-63526-3

Text copyright © 1997  by Julie Sykes.
Illustrations copyright © 1997 by Tim Warnes.
All rights reserved. Published by Scholastic Inc., 555 Broadway,
New York, NY 10012, by arrangement with Little Tiger Press.

SCHOLASTIC and associated logos are trademarks and/or registered trademarks of Scholastic Inc.

12 11 10 9 8 7 6 5 4 3 2 1          8 9/9 0 1 2 3/0

Printed in the U.S.A.          08

First Scholastic printing, September 1998

# I don't want to take a bath!

*by* Julie Sykes

*Pictures by* Tim Warnes

SCHOLASTIC INC.

New York   Toronto   London   Auckland   Sydney

Little Tiger had spent the whole morning playing exciting games. He didn't mean to get dirty, but afterward Mommy Tiger said, "Little Tiger, you need a bath."

"I don't *want* to take a bath!" Little Tiger answered.

"Bathing is fun," said Mommy Tiger, and she took him down to the river to clean him up.

But Little Tiger wouldn't get into the water. "I don't want to take a bath!" he cried again, and he hurried off into the jungle before she could make him.

First Little Tiger visited his favorite friend, Little Monkey. They climbed trees and swung from vines. Little Tiger wasn't as good at climbing as Little Monkey, and when he fell off, his paws became very dirty.

Then Mommy Monkey shouted, "Bath time, Little Monkey, and Little Tiger, too!"

"I don't want to take a bath!" cried Little Tiger, and with a flash of his dirty paws, he scurried past Mommy Monkey toward the bushes.

Next Little Tiger went to play with his old friend, Little Bear. They crawled through the bushes and searched for ripe berries. Little Tiger got berry juice all over his face.

Then Daddy Bear growled, "Bath time,
Little Bear, and Little Tiger, too!"
"I don't want to take a bath!" said Little
Tiger, and twitching his stained whiskers,
he scampered past
Daddy Bear down
to the water hole.

At the water hole Little Tiger met his dear friend, Little Elephant. They started to wrestle, and Little Elephant squirted mud all over Little Tiger's fur.

Then Daddy Elephant trumpeted, "Bath time, Little Elephant, and Little Tiger, too!"

"I don't want to take a bath!" answered Little Tiger, and shaking his muddy coat, he raced past Daddy Elephant toward the grassy plain.

Little Tiger visited his new friend, Little Rhino, next. They charged around in the grass, and Little Tiger got burrs in his tail. Then Mommy Rhino roared, "Bath time, Little Rhino, and Little Tiger, too!"

"I don't want to take a bath!" said Little Tiger, and swishing his tangled tail, he galloped past Mommy Rhino back into the jungle.

"Mommy Tiger will be
wondering where I am," thought
Little Tiger. Knowing he was probably
in trouble, he sadly started for home.
**But wait—what was that?**

Little Tiger looked up
and saw. . .

. . . a handsome peacock showing off his tail.

"How beautiful," gasped Little Tiger. "Will you come play with me?"

The peacock turned up his beak. "Play with you?" he said. "No thanks!"

"Why not?" asked Little Tiger in surprise.

"You're so grubby you would spoil my feathers," said the peacock scornfully. "You need a bath!"
And tossing his head, he strutted off.

"What an awful thing
to say," thought Little Tiger.
"I don't need a bath."

Little Tiger wandered on until he reached the river. Playing with his friends had made him thirsty, and he stopped to have a drink.

"Who's that?" he cried, seeing a reflection in the water. "It can't be me. I'm not *that* dirty."

He leaned over to look more carefully—
and fell right in!

Little Tiger spluttered to the surface.
"It *was* me," he cried. "What a mess I am."
At last Little Tiger took his bath. He splished
and splashed in the warm water. It was fun,
just as Mommy Tiger had said it would be.
Once he was clean, Little Tiger climbed back
onto the bank and admired his reflection.
Wouldn't Mommy Tiger be pleased!

Right then Little Leopard tumbled by. "Hello, Little Tiger," he called. "Will you come play with me?"

Little Tiger looked at Little Leopard's spotted fur and shook his head. "No thanks," he said. "You're so dirty you would spoil my nice shiny coat. You need a bath!"

And with a flick of his clean tail,
Little Tiger hurried home.